The Soggy Doggy

Jenny Kalahar

The author would like to thank all who care for animals and look after their well-being via adoption, medical attention, fostering, volunteering, and office work.

One fine day
after a long, long rain,
I was sitting on my front porch
watching the flowers bloom again,
watching the sky blow clear and sunny,
and watching a squirrel steal seeds from the birdfeeder.

That was when I saw a dog come into my yard.

"Woof woof!"

He was very, very wet,
so I supposed he had been
caught outside during the shower.
"Please," said I, "won't you come here,
you poor, soggy doggy?"

He shook his long, wet fur
until he looked like a sprinkler,
but he did not come any closer.

One fine day
after a long, long rain,
I was sitting on my front porch
when I saw a dog come into my yard.

"Woof woof!"

I noticed that he looked sleepy,
as if he had been walking a very long way
or for a very long time
and could not walk another step.
"Please," I said, "please come here,
you groggy, soggy doggy."

He did not move.

One fine day
after a long, long rain,
I was sitting on my front porch
when I saw a dog come into my yard.

"Woof woof!"

I saw that his brown fur,
though mostly dark from being soaking wet,
had patches that were lighter and darker.

"Please," I said, "please come here to me,
you spotty, groggy, soggy doggy."

He yawned a great, slow yawn, but he did not walk any closer.

One fine day
after a long, long rain,
I was sitting on my front porch
when I saw a dog come into my yard.

"Woof!"

I could tell that he was quite a nice dog, really,
but I teased him for being so standoffish.

"Oh, please," I begged, "please come here to me,
you haughty, naughty, spotty, groggy, soggy doggy."

He yawned again,
looked slightly interested in the squirrel
who was scampering up my tree,
but that was all he did.

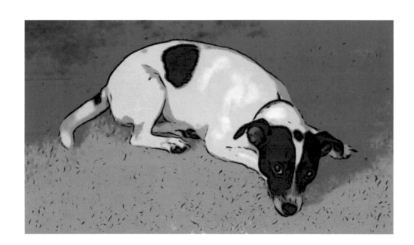

One fine day
after a long, long rain,
I was sitting on my front porch
when I saw a dog come into my yard.

"Woof!"

I noticed then that he was rather thin.
I wondered if it had been a long time since he'd had a bite to eat.
I went into my house, got a slice of sandwich meat,
and then brought it out to the porch where I sat down on the front step.

"Please," I called, "please take this and eat it,
you hungry, haughty, naughty, spotty, groggy, soggy doggy."

He sniffed the air, wagged his tail a little, but would not come near.
He did not even look tempted.
I tossed it to him, and after giving it a thorough sniff
he chomped it and chewed it and swallowed it right down.

One fine day
after a long, long rain,
I was sitting on my front porch step
looking at a dog who had come into my yard.

"Woof woof woof woof!"

He kept on woofing for a moment, and then turned to the squirrel
to excitedly woof some more.
This talkativeness went on and on for quite some time.
I wished I could speak to him to make him understand
that I only wanted to help.

"Please," I said kindly, "please come closer to talk with me,
you flibberty-gibberty, hungry, haughty, naughty, spotty,
groggy, soggy doggy." I paused. "Please!"

He stopped woofing and cocked his wet head at me,
his large, dark eyes seeming to wonder what I would have to say,
and if I could really say anything at all in his language.

One fine day
after a long, long rain,
I was sitting on my front porch step
looking at a dog who had come into my yard.

"Woof!"

Most of his large, dark eyes were covered with long, wet fur.
He actually had long, wet fur all over, and when he wagged his tail
raindrops flicked off the end of it. He really, *really* needed a good trimming.

"Please," I said from my place on my porch step, "please come closer
so I can get the fur out of your eyes, you shaggy-scraggy,
flibberty-gibberty, hungry, haughty, naughty, spotty, groggy, soggy doggy."

Sploosh! flew a few more raindrops as his tail went to and fro.
But he did not come closer. He did not come a single inch toward me at all.

One fine day
after a long, long rain,
I was sitting on my front porch step
looking at a dog who had come into my yard.

"Pah-woof!"

He was really *wet!* I went into my house, into the hall closet
where all sorts of things are kept
and found some old towels I hadn't used in years.

"Please," I said when I'd returned to the porch steps.
"Let me dry you off, you splishy-splashy, shaggy-scraggy,
flibberty-gibberty, hungry, haughty, naughty, spotty, groggy, soggy doggy."
I held out one of the towels invitingly. "Okay?"

He merely moaned and shook himself again.

One fine day
after a long, long rain,
I was sitting on my front porch step
looking at a dog who had come into my yard.

"Pah-woof woof woof!"

This time when he shook himself I thought I heard a faint jingle.
Through the thick fur at his neck I could barely see
that he was wearing a red collar.
"It must have some sort of a bell on it," I thought.
Usually, bells are put on cats' collars, not on dogs',
so this struck me as very, very weird. I listened closely. Yes!
He was, indeed, wearing a little bell.

"Please, my friend," I said as I held both hands out to him,
"please come here and let me see your collar, you ringy-dingy,
splishy-splashy, shaggy-scraggy, flibberty-gibberty, hungry,
haughty, naughty, spotty, groggy, soggy doggy."

He scowled. He turned his head toward the road that runs past my house.
The one with the potholes that were filled with puddles.
He was thinking about running again.

One fine day
after a long, long rain,
I was standing on my front porch step
looking at a dog who had come into my yard.

"Grr-woof!"

I took another step closer to him.
I was getting worried.
He might run out into the road,
and then I would never get close enough to him
so that I could pet his wet, wet head and look at his collar.
His collar that I hoped might have a phone number on it
that I could then call to tell his people that I had their dog.
I didn't move, but *he* did—backward two full steps. He was spooked!

"Please, good boy," I cooed at him, "please don't run away,
you heebie-jeebied, ringy-dingy, splishy-splashy, shaggy-scraggy,
flibberty-gibberty, hungry, haughty, naughty, spotty, groggy, soggy doggy."

He didn't go back another step, but he didn't walk forward, either.

One fine day
after a long, long rain,
I was standing on my front porch step
looking at a dog who had come into my yard.

"Bark!"

I walked down another step, trying to get closer to him.
He was looking at me and didn't notice that the letter carrier
had walked up behind him, her bag of mail over one shoulder.
She was smiling a delightfully happy smile.

"Teddy!" she called. "Teddy! Where have you been?
Your people have been looking all over for you for many days."

Teddy the dog knew the letter carrier's voice.
He turned to her and bounded all around her in circles,
barking and woofing, wagging his tail, the little bell on his collar jingling,
the joy in his heart shining in his large, brown eyes.
The letter carrier took the sack of mail from her shoulder.
She knelt on the damp grass and hugged the
shaggy-scraggy soggy doggy around his spotty neck.

"May I use your phone, please?" the woman asked while still hugging
that wiggly, jiggly dog.
"I know a family who will be so, *so* thrilled to know I've found their Ted!"

Five minutes later, a blue car drove down the road,
avoiding the potholes and puddles as best it could.
It pulled over to the side of the road under a tree
with a chattering squirrel in it who was shaking his tail
and trying to get a better look at what was going to happen.

Three little girls ran from the car,
their arms wide open and their nearly-matching faces as hippety-happety
as they could possibly be. A mother and father followed close behind,
holding hands with each other in a very lovey-dovey way.

Teddy the soggy doggy (who was less soggy after being toweled off
once the mail lady had brought him up onto the porch at last)
leaped from the steps, sped across the yard, and yipped and yapped
as the girls hugged and patted him.

Before I knew what had happened, the dog and his family
were back in their car, zig-zagging around the potholes
and heading for home.

The letter carrier must have seen that my face was sorrowful
after Teddy had gone. She said, "I came across a homeless puppy the other
day on my route. I took him to the shelter. He is a shaggy, brown little guy.
I think he'd love to come right here to your house to live.
What do you think, Miss Rimes?"

One fine day
after a long, long rain,
I was sitting on my front porch watching the flowers bloom again,
watching the sky blow clear and sunny,
and watching a squirrel steal seeds from the birdfeeder.
On my lap was a shaggy brown puppy
who was watching fat rain drops drip from the green green leaves
on the trees, and the squirrel who was inching closer and closer
up the walk toward the front steps.

"Please," I said to Freddy, my own little dog, "let me tell you a true story
of the day I found out about you. About how you needed a home."

I shifted to make us more comfortable, I held him a little higher to my chest,
and then I told him about a very wonderful heebie-jeebied, ringy-dingy,
splishy-splashy, shaggy-scraggy, flibberty-gibberty, hungry, haughty, naughty,
spotty, groggy, soggy doggy.

Freddy looked up at me when I was done telling him all about Teddy.
He winked, licked my cheek, and then flopped his head down onto his paws.
When he did so, the tiny, little bell on his red collar jingled,
and its tinkly-tankly sound from that day until this
always reminds me of the wet, brown dog who I will never, ever forget.

The End

CPSIA information can be obtained
at www.ICGtesting.com
Printed in the USA
BVHW011100090723
666959BV00002B/8

* 9 7 8 1 7 2 7 3 4 3 8 2 3 *